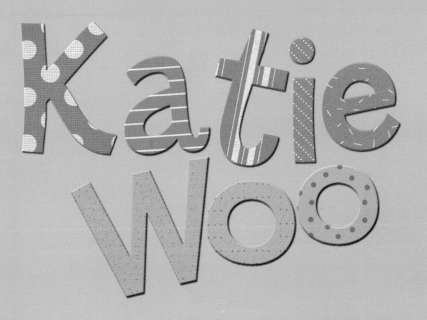

Katie Woo

The Big Lie

by Fran Manushkin

illustrated by Tammie Lyon

raintree

Raintree is an imprint of Capstone Global Library Limited, a company
incorporated in England and Wales having its registered office at 264 Banbury
Road, Oxford, OX2 7DY – Registered company number: 6695582

www.raintree.co.uk
myorders@raintree.co.uk

Text © Capstone Global Library Limited 2019
The moral rights of the proprietor have been asserted.

Creative Director: Heather Kindseth
Graphic Designer: Emily Harris
Printed and bound in India
ISBN 978 1 4747 8221 0
23 22 21 20 19
10 9 8 7 6 5 4 3 2 1

British Library Cataloguing in Publication Data
A full catalogue record for this book is available from the British Library.

Acknowledgements
Fran Manushkin, pg. 26
Tammie Lyon, pg. 26

Contents

Chapter 1
The missing plane

One day after break,

Miss Winkle told the class,

"Jake has lost his toy

aeroplane. Has anyone

seen it?"

Katie Woo
shook her head.
So did her
friends Pedro
and JoJo and
everyone else.

"My father gave me
the plane yesterday,"
said Jake.

"It was a birthday
present," he said.

"Maybe your plane flew
away," said someone else.

"That's not funny," said
Miss Winkle.

JoJo told Jake, "I saw you playing with your plane at break. It's cool! I hope you find it."

Miss Winkle asked again,

"Does anyone know where

Jake's aeroplane is?"

"I don't," Katie told Jake.

But she was lying.

Chapter 2
Katie's bad grab

Earlier that day during break, Katie saw Jake running around with his aeroplane.

"I want to do that!" Katie told herself. "I wish that plane belonged to me."

When break was nearly

over, three fire engines sped

past.

While everyone was

watching them and waving

to the firefighters, Katie

grabbed Jake's

plane. She put it

in her pocket.

Now Jake's plane was
inside Katie's desk.

"I can't wait to play with
it when I get home," Katie
thought.

During art class, Katie said, "Maybe a kangaroo hopped over and put the plane in her pouch."

"I don't think so," said Miss Winkle. "There are no kangaroos around here."

During spelling, Katie said, "Maybe the rubbish collectors came and took Jake's plane."

"No way!" JoJo said. She shook her head. "I didn't see any bin lorries."

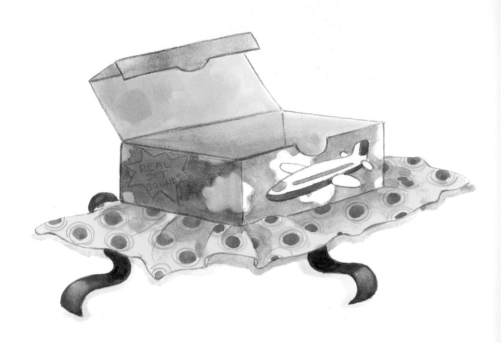

Jake kept staring at
the empty box that his
aeroplane came in. The
birthday ribbon was still on
the box.

Jake looked like he was
going to cry.

Katie didn't feel happy either.

When nobody was looking, she took something out of her desk and put it in her pocket.

Chapter 3
The truth

Katie walked to the

window and began using

the pencil sharpener.

All of a sudden, Katie yelled, "I see Jake's plane. It's by the window! It must have flown in during break."

Katie handed Jake the
plane. She whispered, "That
was a lie, Jake. I took your
plane, and I'm very sorry!"

At first, Jake was angry at Katie. Then he said, "I'm glad you gave it back. I feel a lot better now."

"I do too!" Katie said.

And that was the truth.

About the author

Fran Manushkin is the author of many popular picture books, including *Baby, Come Out!*; *Latkes and Applesauce: A Hanukkah Story*; *The Belly Book* and *Big Girl Panties*. There is a real Katie Woo - she's Fran's great-niece - but she never gets in half the trouble that Katie Woo does in the books. Fran writes on her beloved Mac computer in New York City, USA, without the help of her two naughty cats, Chaim and Goldy.

About the illustrator

Tammie Lyon's love for drawing began at a young age while sitting at the kitchen table with her dad. She continued her love of art and eventually attended college, where she earned a bachelors degree in fine art. After a brief career as a professional ballet dancer, she decided to devote herself full time to illustration. Today she lives with her husband, Lee, in Cincinnati, Ohio, USA. Her dogs, Gus and Dudley, keep her company as she works in her studio.

 # Glossary

either also

empty nothing inside

kangaroo an animal that lives in Australia

lying saying something that's not true

sharpener an item that is used to make something sharper

Discussion questions

1. Katie was jealous of Jake. She wanted his aeroplane for herself. Have you ever been jealous of someone?

2. Katie lied to Jake. Has anyone ever lied to you? How did it make you feel?

3. The teacher did not find out that Katie took the plane. What do you think would have happened if the teacher found out?

Writing prompts

1. Katie broke some rules in the story. Write down at least one rule that she broke.

2. Katie said that a kangaroo might have taken the aeroplane. Draw a picture of a kangaroo with the plane, and write a sentence about your kangaroo.

3. Katie apologized for taking the plane. Pretend you need to apologize for something, and write a letter to say you are sorry.

In this book, Katie Woo told a big lie. Everyone knows that lying is wrong. But with this game, you can tell lies and nobody will get hurt.

The Truth and Lies game

Play this game with a group of friends or classmates.

1. Each player needs a piece of paper and a pen or pencil.

2. Each player writes down three things about themselves. You could share your favourite things, best holiday places or hobbies. But one thing should be true and two things should be lies.

3. Take turns reading out loud your lists of three things. After all three items have been read out, the group votes on which item is true. When the vote is complete, the reader tells the group which one is true.

You are sure to learn lots of fun things about your friends!

WAIT!

DON'T CLOSE THE BOOK!

THERE'S MORE!

FIND MORE BOOKS YOU'LL LOVE

AT...

www.RAINTREE.co.uk